In the
PALACE
of the
OCEAN KING

In the
Palace
of the
Ocean King

by Marilyn Singer

illustrated by Ted Rand

ATHENEUM BOOKS FOR YOUNG READERS

Two things were said of Lord Adelbert's daughter, Mariana: She feared nothing but the ocean, and she had never been in love. Both things were true.

One fine day the lord took her to visit his old friend, a duke who lived in a great but gloomy castle by the sea. Dinner that night might have been a dismal affair if Mariana had not brightened the table with her clever stories.

When she finished the last, the duke turned to the quiet young man sitting by his side. "My son can tell a good tale too, can you not, Sylvain?"

"Can you? Then tell us your favorite," Mariana begged with a dazzling smile.

Sylvain lowered his eyes. All evening he had looked at nothing and no one but Mariana, but now he could not look at her at all. Nor could he utter a word until his father prodded him once again. Then in a mumble he began.

"There was a young man who went walking on the beach. He saw a merman stranded there, feebly thrashing his tail. The creature's eyes were dull and glazed, and his voice was so weak that the youth had to lay his ear close to the merman's cracked lips to hear him.

" 'Because I would not do his bidding, I angered the mighty Ocean King,' the merman said. 'With his triton he stirred the waters and threw me from the sea. Now only a human can take me back. Will you be the one?'

"The young man took pity on the creature, for he had heard of the fearsome Ocean King and he believed the merman's tale. So, although the sand was wet, the creature was heavy, and the youth had to struggle long and hard, he at last placed the merman back into the sea, where a mermaid who was weeping welcomed him with joy and great relief. 'I will not forget your kindness,' the merman called to the youth. 'I will help you and your beloved if you ever are in need.' "

Sylvain abruptly stopped speaking.

His father frowned. "That is all?" he asked, for he liked to laugh or be made to shiver, and he found this story neither witty nor chilling. "Your tale has no ending. Did the merman help the lad?"

"Not yet," muttered Sylvain.

Mariana stared uneasily at him. "You speak as if the tale were true."

"It is," he replied.

She felt a wave of cold go up her spine. But she quickly laughed it away. Then Sylvain blushed, bent his head, and busied himself with the food left on his plate. He did not speak another word the whole evening long.

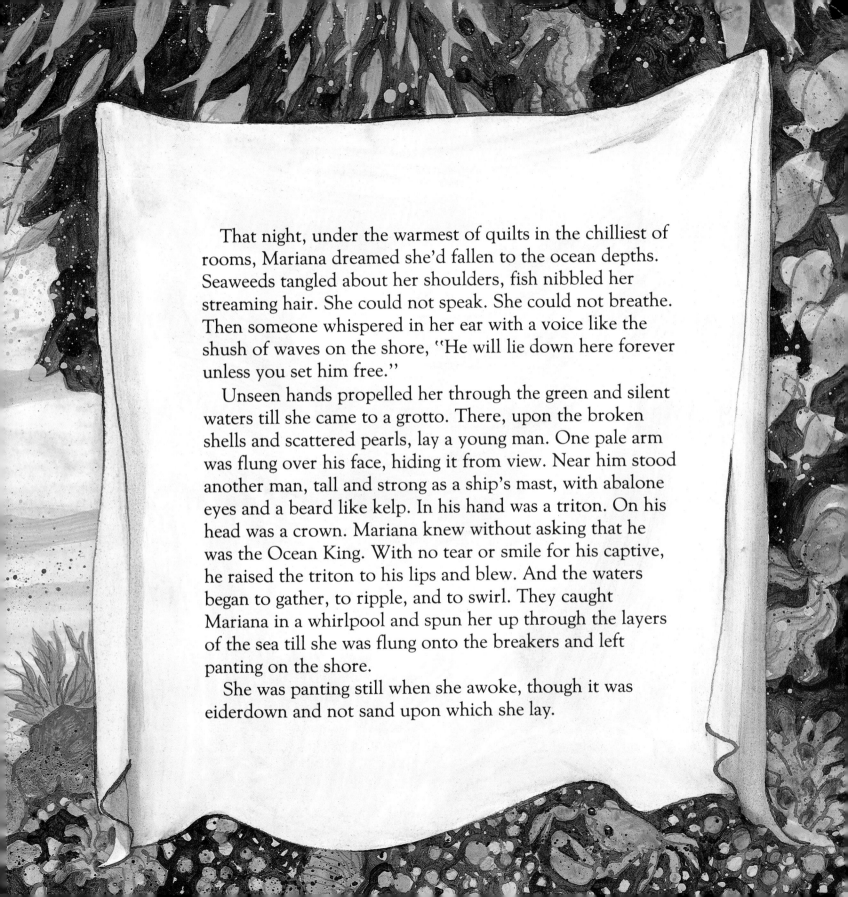

That night, under the warmest of quilts in the chilliest of rooms, Mariana dreamed she'd fallen to the ocean depths. Seaweeds tangled about her shoulders, fish nibbled her streaming hair. She could not speak. She could not breathe. Then someone whispered in her ear with a voice like the shush of waves on the shore, "He will lie down here forever unless you set him free."

Unseen hands propelled her through the green and silent waters till she came to a grotto. There, upon the broken shells and scattered pearls, lay a young man. One pale arm was flung over his face, hiding it from view. Near him stood another man, tall and strong as a ship's mast, with abalone eyes and a beard like kelp. In his hand was a triton. On his head was a crown. Mariana knew without asking that he was the Ocean King. With no tear or smile for his captive, he raised the triton to his lips and blew. And the waters began to gather, to ripple, and to swirl. They caught Mariana in a whirlpool and spun her up through the layers of the sea till she was flung onto the breakers and left panting on the shore.

She was panting still when she awoke, though it was eiderdown and not sand upon which she lay.

In the days that followed she told no one of her dream, not her father, not the duke, and not even Sylvain, in whose company she was more and more to be found—standing on the ramparts, sitting in the courtyard, strolling through the castle, but never by the sea. He still spoke very little, but it seemed to her he said so much, and each day she rose ever more eager to be at his side again.

But one evening as they sat by the fire in the Great Hall, he told her in his shy and halting voice that the next day he would be sailing far across the waters to a land he'd never seen. Mariana's heart grew as heavy as the iron chest her father kept in his room. Yet she did not tell Sylvain of her grief.

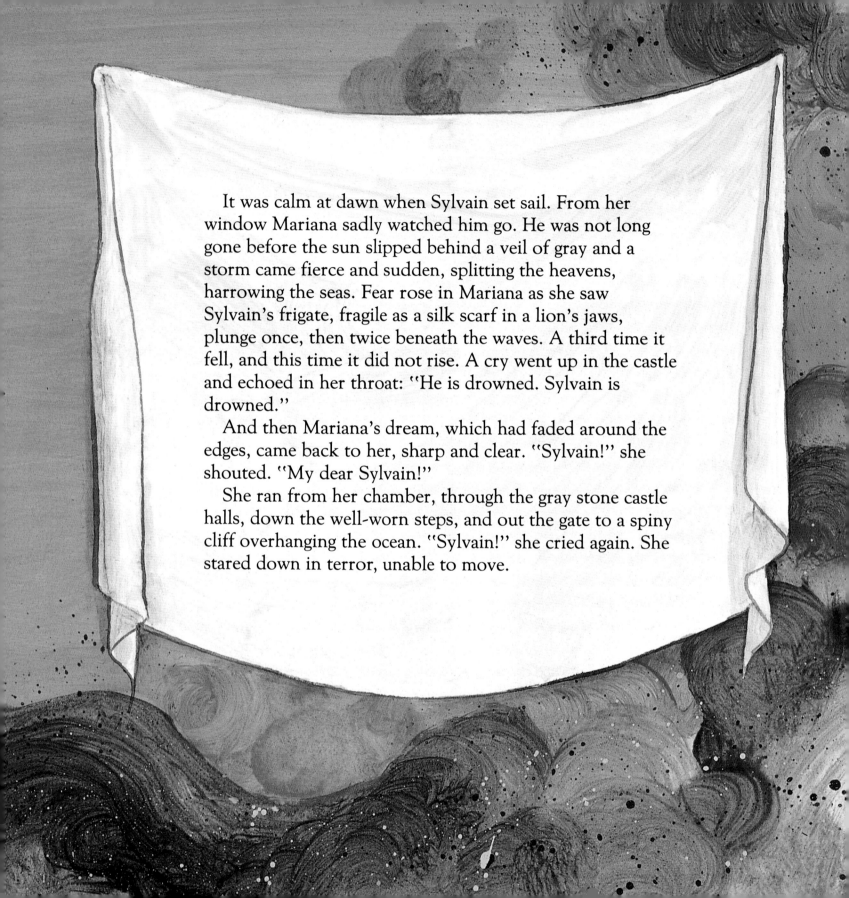

It was calm at dawn when Sylvain set sail. From her window Mariana sadly watched him go. He was not long gone before the sun slipped behind a veil of gray and a storm came fierce and sudden, splitting the heavens, harrowing the seas. Fear rose in Mariana as she saw Sylvain's frigate, fragile as a silk scarf in a lion's jaws, plunge once, then twice beneath the waves. A third time it fell, and this time it did not rise. A cry went up in the castle and echoed in her throat: "He is drowned. Sylvain is drowned."

And then Mariana's dream, which had faded around the edges, came back to her, sharp and clear. "Sylvain!" she shouted. "My dear Sylvain!"

She ran from her chamber, through the gray stone castle halls, down the well-worn steps, and out the gate to a spiny cliff overhanging the ocean. "Sylvain!" she cried again. She stared down in terror, unable to move.

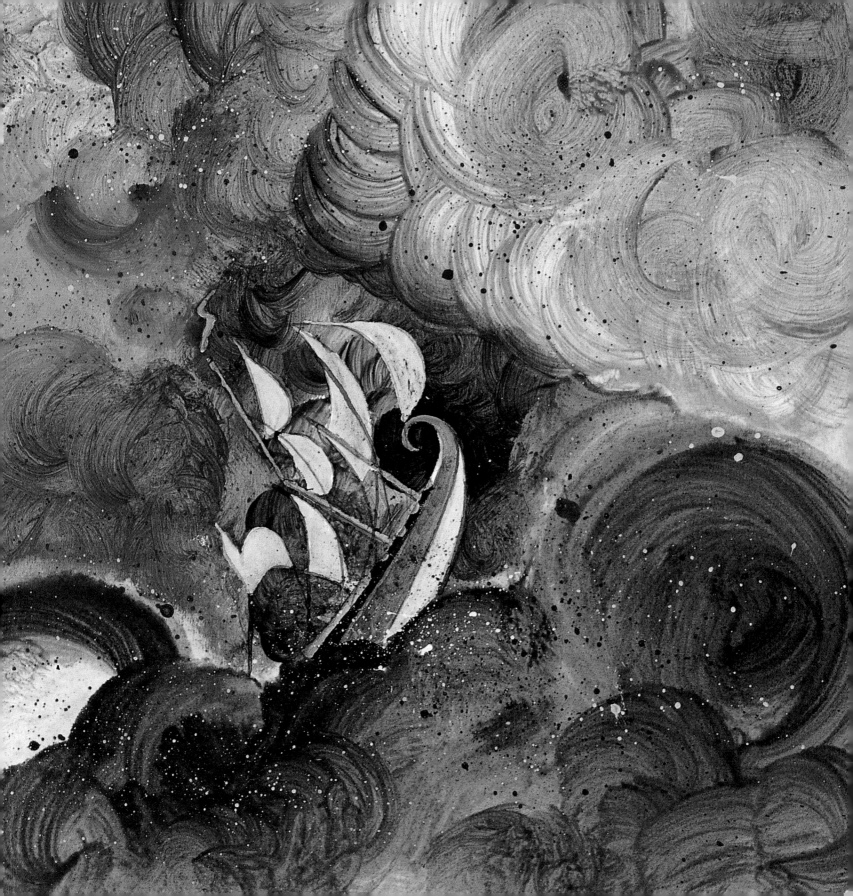

Then up through the waves rose the merman. He called to Mariana in a voice like the shush of surf upon the sand: "The Ocean King has your Sylvain. He will keep him forever unless you set him free."

"Tell me how," Mariana begged.

"If I tell you, you must follow."

"I will follow," she agreed, with dread.

"You must dive into the sea, all the way down to the Ocean King's palace. There you must seize the king's triton—he cannot wrest it from a living hand—and with it barter for your young man's life."

Mariana shuddered. "That is the only way?"

"The only way," the merman replied. "You must do it now—before it is too late."

Mariana trembled so that she could hardly stand. Her teeth rattled like wind-tossed shells. I cannot do this thing, she thought, not even to save my dear Sylvain. Then she saw as if in a glass his face upon the water. Crying out his name, she stretched out her arms and plunged into the roiling sea.

Down she sank like an anchor,
scattering fish and dragging seaweed in
her wake, to depths where chimaeras
with glowing eyes and gleaming jaws
brushed her sides and were gone. All
this way the merman stayed by her side.
At last they came to the grotto, and by
its strange light they saw Sylvain lying
cold and white as whalebone upon its
pearly floor. Over him stood the Ocean
King, the triton hanging from a golden
chain about his massive neck.

"Give him back to me," Mariana
tried to say. But she could not breathe
and she could not speak.

The king passed his palms over Sylvain's closed eyes. The young man rose, swaying like a reed. Then the king clapped his hands. The grotto's bottom shifted, and stairs came into view. Up those steps came the Ocean King's servants. Two held a net like a mantle. Four bore the king's own chair. The king beckoned to the servants with the net. They came forward, draped it over Sylvain's shoulders, then stepped back. The king made another motion with his hand, and this time it was Sylvain who glided toward him, then turned and moved weightlessly down the dark stairs. The two servants followed, and then the king himself on his golden chair.

"You must go too," the merman whispered in Mariana's ear. "I cannot, but you must....Quickly now—before he joins the dance."

And quickly she went, clinging to the shadows so that she would not be seen. Through corridors of black coral she followed the king and his men till they came to his silver-scaled palace. Inside its walls, where the air was clear and sweet, there was a ballroom with ninety-nine guests, some in velvet, some in rags, all with hollow cheeks and sunken eyes. The guests were moving in the circles of a slow and endless waltz. Only when the king clapped his hands did they stop. Then they drifted into rows, the men in one, the women in another, and stood staring across the room with unseeing eyes. The last to join the line was the hundredth guest, Sylvain.

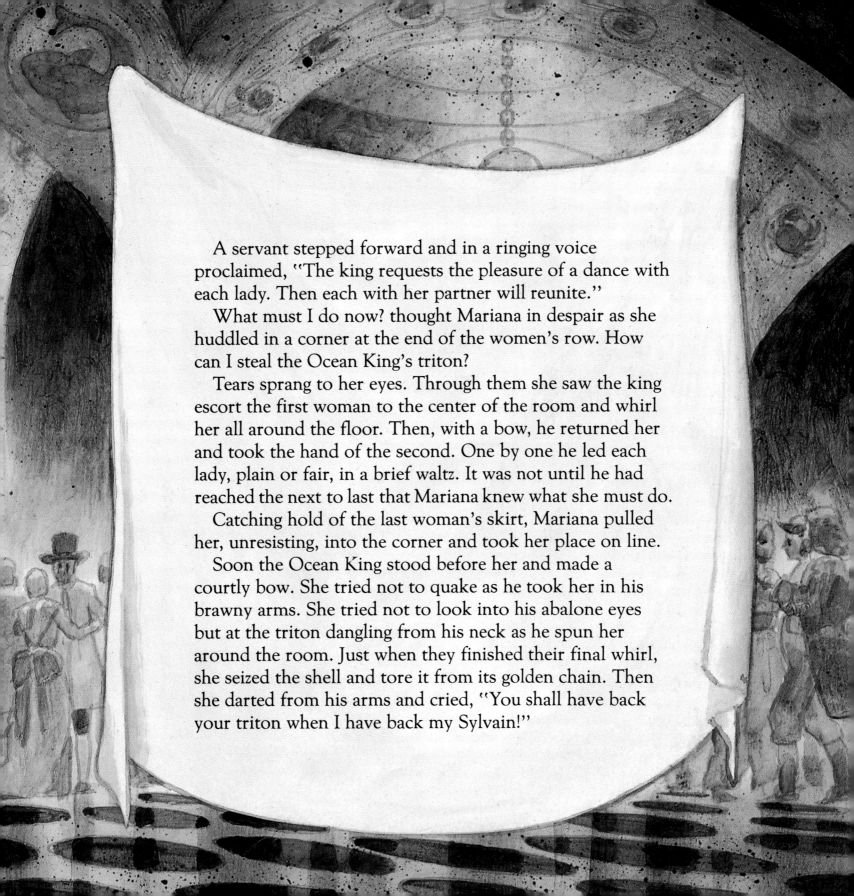

A servant stepped forward and in a ringing voice proclaimed, "The king requests the pleasure of a dance with each lady. Then each with her partner will reunite."

What must I do now? thought Mariana in despair as she huddled in a corner at the end of the women's row. How can I steal the Ocean King's triton?

Tears sprang to her eyes. Through them she saw the king escort the first woman to the center of the room and whirl her all around the floor. Then, with a bow, he returned her and took the hand of the second. One by one he led each lady, plain or fair, in a brief waltz. It was not until he had reached the next to last that Mariana knew what she must do.

Catching hold of the last woman's skirt, Mariana pulled her, unresisting, into the corner and took her place on line.

Soon the Ocean King stood before her and made a courtly bow. She tried not to quake as he took her in his brawny arms. She tried not to look into his abalone eyes but at the triton dangling from his neck as he spun her around the room. Just when they finished their final whirl, she seized the shell and tore it from its golden chain. Then she darted from his arms and cried, "You shall have back your triton when I have back my Sylvain!"

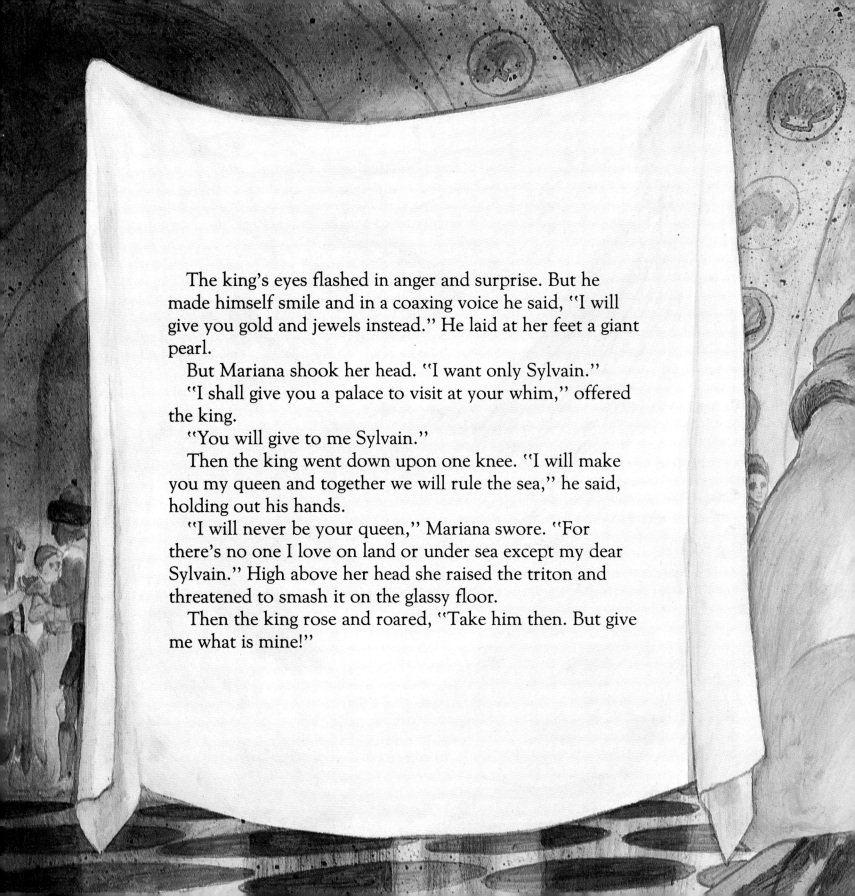

The king's eyes flashed in anger and surprise. But he made himself smile and in a coaxing voice he said, "I will give you gold and jewels instead." He laid at her feet a giant pearl.

But Mariana shook her head. "I want only Sylvain."

"I shall give you a palace to visit at your whim," offered the king.

"You will give to me Sylvain."

Then the king went down upon one knee. "I will make you my queen and together we will rule the sea," he said, holding out his hands.

"I will never be your queen," Mariana swore. "For there's no one I love on land or under sea except my dear Sylvain." High above her head she raised the triton and threatened to smash it on the glassy floor.

Then the king rose and roared, "Take him then. But give me what is mine!"

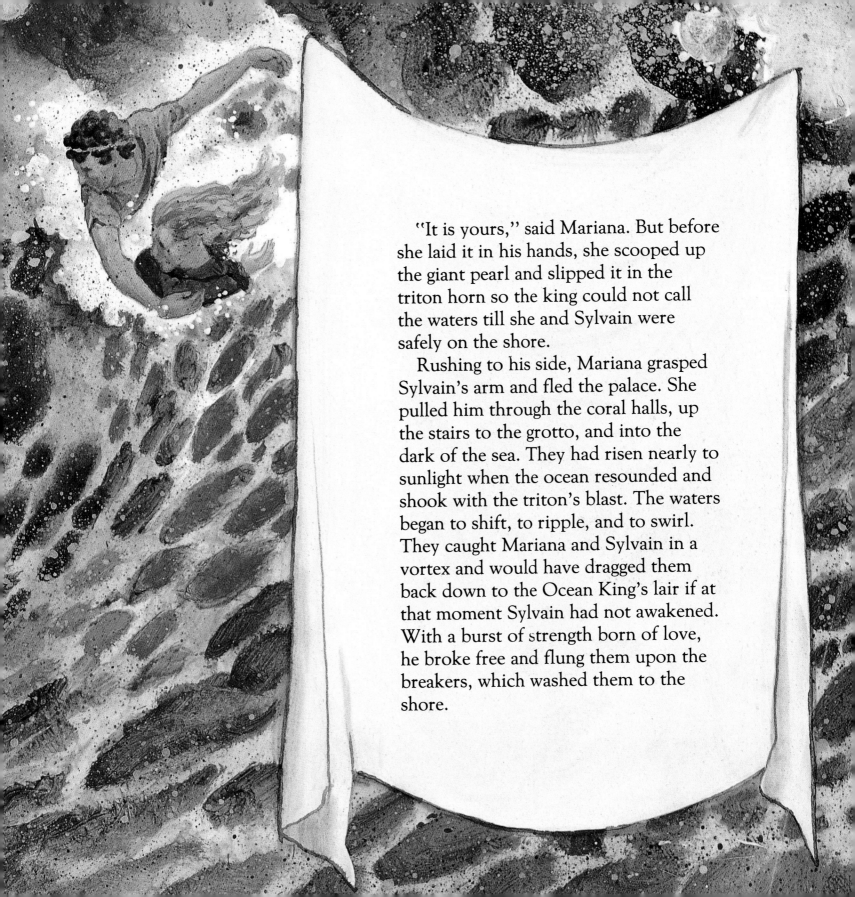

"It is yours," said Mariana. But before she laid it in his hands, she scooped up the giant pearl and slipped it in the triton horn so the king could not call the waters till she and Sylvain were safely on the shore.

Rushing to his side, Mariana grasped Sylvain's arm and fled the palace. She pulled him through the coral halls, up the stairs to the grotto, and into the dark of the sea. They had risen nearly to sunlight when the ocean resounded and shook with the triton's blast. The waters began to shift, to ripple, and to swirl. They caught Mariana and Sylvain in a vortex and would have dragged them back down to the Ocean King's lair if at that moment Sylvain had not awakened. With a burst of strength born of love, he broke free and flung them upon the breakers, which washed them to the shore.

It was some time before they could rise. But at last they did, and then embraced. They were embracing still when Lord Adelbert and the duke found them there. All the bells of the castle were made to peal, the cannons to thunder, the trumpets to blare; and so they would again a few months hence on the lovers' wedding day.

Then Mariana said to Sylvain, "Your tale has at last an ending."

"And a beginning," he replied, gazing full into her eyes.

They smiled radiantly at each other, for they knew both things were true.

To Joe, Nora, Hopi, Ara, and Seta

—M. S.

To my granddaughter Sierra

—T. R.

Acknowledgments

Thanks to Steve Aronson and Meredith Charpentier,
and to my editor, Jonathan Lanman

—M. S.

Atheneum Books for Young Readers
An imprint of Simon & Schuster Children's Publishing Division
1230 Avenue of the Americas, New York, NY 10020

Text copyright © 1995 by Marilyn Singer
Illustrations copyright © 1995 by Ted Rand

First edition
The text of this book is set in Goudy Old Style.
The illustrations are rendered in ink, bamboo pen, and acrylic paints.
Printed in the United States of America
10 9 8 7 6 5 4 3 2 1

Library of Congress Cataloging-in-Publication Data

Singer, Marilyn.
    In the palace of the Ocean King / by Marilyn Singer ; illustrated
by Ted Rand. — 1st ed.
        p.   cm.
    Summary: An original fairy tale in which the daughter of a Lord
overcomes her fear of the ocean when she rescues her beloved from
the Ocean King.
    ISBN 0-689-31755-7
    [1. Fairy tales.] I. Rand, Ted, ill. II. title.
PZ8.S3576In   1995
[E]—dc20   94-12778